DreamScape

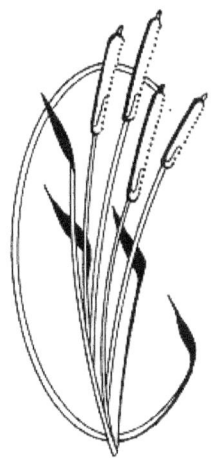

DreamScape

by

Joshua Jeremiah Hill

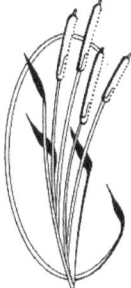

Senior Publisher
Steven Lawrence Hill Sr.

Awarded Publishing House
ASA Publishing Company

ASA Publishing Company
An Accredited Publishing House by the BBB
105 E. Front St., Suite. 101, Monroe, Michigan 48161
www.asapublishingcompany.com

Copyrights©2013 Joshua Jeremiah Hill, All Rights Reserved
Book: DreamScape
Date Published: 11.22.2013
Edition 1   - *Trade Paperback*
Book ASAPCID: 2380632
ISBN: 978-1-886528-71-0
Library of Congress Cataloging-in-Publication Data

This book was published in the United States of America.
State of Michigan

A Publisher Trademark Title page

WELCOME TO

DREAMSCAPE

Short Fantasy Stories

Table of Contents

Broken Tradition 1

Old Wounds 7

One Disciple 15

The Horseman 23

War Machine 33

DreamScape

by

Joshua Jeremiah Hill

Broken Tradition

The rain beaded off his chest-plate as he walked further into the forum. The Greek Architecture was beautiful and astounding. A marvel to behold in one's eye. It was a true shame it was tarnished by the presence of 'him.' The dark magic created a barrier so he couldn't get wet.

A S A   P u b l i s h i n g   C o m p a n y

2 | Joshua Jeremiah Hill

"Oh! The great and powerful Zeus has returned to do what?!"

"You should have killed me Hades. Now you must face me."

Twisted laughter spewed from his mouth. "My, my, Zeus how harmless you look from up here. It's like looking at a bug."

"You shall pay for your insolence!" The blast that was meant for Hades was deflected. The war axe wasn't marked at all by the blast.

Ares jumped down in front of Zeus, "Hello father." His heavy dark-grey armor had silver accents in it.

"Why did you ever help Hades?!"

"He proved more of a father than you ever did!"

Dark energy slammed Zeus backwards.

"Uranus slayed by Cronus, Cronus slayed by Zeus. Now, Zeus will be slain by Ares."

"Not today."

A void sword formed in his hand. It seemed like a tradition for the son to kill the father. The two gods rushed each other and their blades met. The mortals looked up at the heavens wondering what was happening. Ares was more chaotic in battle than any other Olympian. He was still lethal non-the-less. Ares slung his axe at Zeus and back to his hand. A volley of energy blasts bombarded Ares. That was a mere distraction so Zeus could get close enough. The attack was refined and well placed. The blows were heavy and would kill a mere mortal. Ares jarred and jolted at the relentless chain of attacks. Hades sat forward in great interest, his pawn could possibly fail him.

Zeus grabbed his lower leg and tossed the War-God to the ground. Zeus wielded his sword back-handed and prepared to finish his son. Hades scrapped forward on the armrest and hands of the underworld pushed his brother back.

"I can't have you killing Ares now can I?"

Undead Spartan Warriors tore through the floor of the forum and clawed to the surface. Guarded by the warriors, Ares jumped back up to where Hades sat. It was a good breather for Zeus to deal with the Spartans. He only had to use little effort to destroy them. He slashed the final Spartan into the air and shocked him with lightning. The corpses were sent back to the underworld. The axe sliced by his head and boomeranged back to Ares. He slammed into the ground bashing Zeus. The regal opponent recovered quickly and fired a blast. Ares caught the blast and threw it back. The explosion kicked up dust obscuring their vision. Hades and Ares peered into the dust to see if anything remained.

Suddenly, a void sword sliced through the dust and knocked the axe from his hand. "Ah!" he shouted. Blast after blast pushed him closer to the edge of the forum until a follow-up punch knocked him off. He wasn't finished there, Zeus bounded over the edge in pursuit of his son. Ares took the full impact as they continued their descent through the crisp air. The two gods grappled and punched one another as they fell towards the earth. He should have known that father and son would be battling over the throne of Olympus. Zeus pulled Ares towards him and electrocuted him. He retaliated with an energy blast that knocked his father against the rocks. A big chunk broke off and fell with them. Zeus grabbed the rock and hurled it. Ares, using dark energy, slowed the rock down and threw it back. A fist full of lightning obliterated the massive rock and they grappled once more.

It was a hellish dawn for the mortal world. Some of them were out and about while others still rested. The humans had no idea the gods were battling. They heard the rumors of Athens being attacked by the undead Spartans. They even heard the Goddess Athena appeared to help her city. So should it be a surprise to see two bright 'stars' fall from the heavens? A sharp cracking sound was heard. All who could see looked and gazed upon the sky. They could see the golden-burning figures descend upon their world. The mortals watched as father and son crashed into the city of Rome.

One landed on the seaport and the other splashed into the water.

"*It's Zeus!*"

"*Why is he among us?*"

"Who was the other that fell?!"

"The world is coming to an end?!"

The mortals couldn't comprehend what was going on. The gods battling was the 'end' to them. It was their religion, their way of life. So yes their world was coming to an end. Ares was sprung from the water splitting a ship into pieces. He smashed one human under his feet and flung another. "If you're going to kill me, you must try much harder."

Sword and axe met once more, the humans fled in terror. A series of jabs and slashes were dealt on both ends. Zeus ripped his helmet off and kicked him back. The attacks were brutal and took their toll on both warriors. They caught each other's weapon-hand and they head butted each other. Zeus fell back and received a strike across his chest-plate. He grabbed a pot and smashed it on Ares' head. The grip loosened on his axe, it was knocked from his hand. The War-God was vulnerable and open for attack. Ares realized this too late. The sword was stained by his golden blood.

His eyes glazed over and blood trickled from his mouth. The mortals gathered to look upon the dying god. Bewilderment took hold as they watched.

"I guess that tradition has been broken. This son won't kill his father." He wiped some blood from his chin. The dark-gray armor was fading of its true color. Those red eyes no longer burned with hatred.

"You should have never joined Hades." The sword he once held now disappeared.

Ares spewed a blood-curdling laugh at his father. "My failure will prove to be the birthmother to success. Zeus, you will meet your end. Someone, something, will rise just to destroy you and all who are faithful. It is just a matter of time...."

Ares' corpse turned into dust and was swept away by the wind. Mortals whispered to one another about the Lightning God. The helmet that rested upon the now deceased god lay on the ground. It burned into a white-hot orb and was placed somewhere special. The game they played was so twisted that father and son aspired to kill one another. He could think of only one who caused this to happen. That black armor and cape accompanied by that infernal helm. That terrible pitchfork that helped the betrayal. The same one who took his throne, "Hades!!!!" His subjects fell to the ground with their faces in the dirt. Zeus coursed with lightning fueled by hatred and pain. The Lightning God erupted into the sky. The sharp cracking sound was heard by all. He soared through the clouds and lightning. The crisp-cool air tightened his lungs. Breath-taking! No one could stop Zeus if they tried. Now Hades has to finish what he started.

Old Wounds

The man stood at a 6'2'' height with a rather athletic build. He could be at an estimated weight of 210'lbs, all muscle. Facial hair was a good five o'clock shadow accompanied with a mustache and a couple scars as well. His black shoulder-length hair was pushed back behind his ears as he listened in on the world revolving around him. His clothing seemed to be a hybrid of the western world where he comes from and the always fashionable Paris. His pants were of a tighter-fit then most men were comfortable with. They were neatly tucked into his riding boots that were a good fit for him. The black blazer was matched with a black vest and white shirt underneath. A flat, wide brimmed hat covered his head. At times the wide brim would produce a shadow over his brown eyes. One should say brown eye because his left eye was now covered by an eye patch. All thanks to a certain somebody.

"Krestel, I presume? I am Jonathan Williamson." Jonathan held out a hand waiting for one in return.

The American looked at his hand and looked at the man. "I'm sorry friend, but you're going to have to earn that."

Jonathan nodded his head and gestured for Krestel to follow. Jonathan showed the tickets and they proceeded into the opera house. They took their seats in the booth and waited. The house was a piece of architect genius. The designs and the importance in every detail were beyond expectations.

His hand twitched, "a gunslinger non-the-less."

"What makes you say that?"

"It was the twitching of your hand. Only a man who has extensive use in firearms would cause such an effect."

"A good observation of you friend," Krestel said, "You know who I am but I know little about you."

"That is for another time, I spotted the one we're looking for."

Bradford was seen in his seat, third row from the front.

"Right there."

"Irene can't be too far behind." Jonathan was right she wasn't too far behind.

"She's getting up, probably going to use the lavatory."

Williamson took off his hat sat it down near his chair. "Let us step too my dear chap."

Krestel snatched his arm before he could move any further. The iron grip had an icy feel that crept up his arm. "You don't know Bradford."

He pointed at his eye patch. "I do, Bradford doesn't travel alone."

Bradford also moved from his seat and followed suit. The hallway where the bathrooms were located was dark and dimly lit. Irene entered the lavatory and was closely followed by Bradford. "Can't you read, that's women only," Krestel said.

"I wonder who they would send after me. The last time I saw you, you were bleeding in the harsh sun, Bradford jarred."

"I'm not the one who's going to bleed friend."

"Come now Krestel you don't think I would travel alone do you?"

Six assassins appeared out of thin air, "Similar to you Krestel?"

"Have fun boys," he disappeared into the bathroom.

The two unlikely allies went to work quickly. Their fighting styles were different but they were practiced and refined. Williamson was shorter than his counter-part, so he had the advantage of agility and speed. His reach was shorter so rapid punches mixed with an unorthodox fighting style made him a very dangerous opponent. Krestel was quick when he needed to be. His height helped and hindered him. The height came with a longer reach that gave him distance advantage. He needs space so his blows can build good enough momentum to do damage. Krestel put his whole body into the punches and kicks that proved devastating. Williamson had a light and rapid approach that considered precision more than damage. Krestel was the heavy-hitter and his punches do great damage.

Williamson executed a 'shut-down' combo that required succession of blows to key areas that would render their body useless. He pushed one assassin to Krestel who delivered a haymaker to his face. One of them tackled Krestel into the bathroom. He kicked him off, grabbed his head, and slammed it into the mirror, then the sink. The last two ganged up on Holmes. They pulled out their daggers and prepared to attack. Krestel kicked one man into the wall as he body slammed the other.

"Oh the savagery!" said Williamson.

All of the assassins were dealt with and they rushed into the bathroom. The scene inside was worst than the one outside in the hallway. The sink was smashed with blood dripping to the floor. Parts of the wall was punched out and the pieces laid on the floor. There was dust in certain other areas in the bathroom. Williamson looked out into the hallway to see that the assassins were gone.

"Where did they go?"

Krestel shook his head, "they're gone by now. Assassins tend to move quickly, stick to the shadows."

Williamson looked upon the man. "It's what we are based on."

He handed Jonathan some tobacco that had been on the floor. "Hmmm, I know this tobacco, it's very strong."

He continued to examine the dust in the specific areas. "Take a look at this. The dust here is different from the dust near the wall and the pieces. This dust is the result of some exterior source."

"So we're looking for a warehouse that contains this specific tobacco."

Jonathan patted Krestel on the shoulder, "precisely."

Jonathan retrieved his hat and they searched the best places Bradford could be. "While we wait for our next destination, would our dear friend like to fill us in?"

Krestel looked at the short man with little interest in the topic. "Bradford and I were partners long ago. We were the best they had to offer. One day something inside him just snapped and he went off the deep-end."

Williamson wanted to ask about the reference Bradford said about their last encounter but didn't. He could tell it was personal. "What does he want with Irene Kooler?"

Krestel shifted in his seat, "Irene stole a certain journal that held important information," he continued, "This is why I'm here, to make sure he doesn't get that journal."

The duo finally arrived at the warehouse and they immediately started to search the place. "Those friends of his Krestel, will there be more?"

"You better hope not, Krestel said."

He spoke to soon. Assassins appeared with mauser pistols. They weren't trying to use words. The two of them dove for cover as the Assassins opened fire. The sixth chamber was empty, only during a gunfight does one load the sixth chamber. The rounds pinged off their cover as they formulated a plan.

Williamson managed to get two shots off, "revolvers against automatics?!"

"The odds are against us but we have seen even worst times." Jonathan slumped down further to avoid the bullets.

"Krestel what do you propose?"

Krestel has disappeared and it was just Williamson in this gun battle.

"Krestel!"

One Disciple

Two berserkers; very large drones that use hammers, and twenty swordsmen appeared. Cat armed her scythe as Lazarus' fist sparked. "I'll take the berserkers, you deal with the swordsmen."

"Don't tell me what to do."

He sighed, "Have it your way."

Both factions rushed towards each other. Cat unleashed energy waves until crossing blades. Lazarus jumped into the air, flipped three times, and planted two feet in the berserker's chest. He then fired a bolt at the berserker. Cat decapitated two swordsmen and heaved her scythe into another one. She barrel-rolled over a swordsman and cut him in two. Lazarus dodged the hammer and shaded towards them. One berserker dashed backwards evading the blow, "what?"

The other dropped his hammer on Lazarus. He was nearly crushed under the force of the blow. He was then hurled into a building. It toppled when the man impacted. Cat killed the final swordsman as Lazarus climbed from the rubble. "Having trouble?"

"Shut up and fight."

The two of them rushed the berserkers. Lazarus performed his burning flare technique blinding the berserker and then tackled it to the ground. His powerful hands collapsed on the berserker's head and fried its brain. Cat worked her way behind the berserker and lifted it off the ground. "Lazarus!"

He was dumbfounded for a second. Lazarus didn't know how much stronger Cat became, but that's for another time. The lighting fist technique destroyed the berserker's face. Its massive body fell lifelessly to the ground. "I didn't know your puny arms could lift such a weight."

Cat looked at him degradingly, "I didn't know berserkers could smack you around like that."

His smirk vanished after that remark. "Aha, aha, don't make me laugh."

A swift current blew through the alley. Two VTOL's arrived with their lasers pointed at Cat and Lazarus. "Lazarus and Cat come quietly."

"I don't think so."

Cat leaped to one building and then hijacked a VTOL. Lazarus flew straight through the other one severing the cockpit. The body of the aircraft crashed into an apartment as the cockpit crackled and sparked as it fell into the alley below. The pilot hit a button calling for back-up. Lazarus ripped the cockpit open and grabbed the pilot. His grip was crushing the man's throat. Desperately gasping for air he pleaded to Lazarus to let go. "Disciple, where is he?"

Lazarus loosened his grip so he could speak, "The tower, he's at the top of the tower."

"Any security protocols we need to know about?"

Lazarus tightened his grip once more. "The entire tower is locked down with troopers on every floor. There are barriers meant for you."

"You're telling me quite a lot."

"I'm not expecting you to live."

"VTOL's, six of them!" Lazarus fused the pilot with lightning and threw him at a VTOL, exploding on impact. Cat took down two more, leaving only three. She strafed to the left and took out another VTOL. Lazarus grabbed one VTOL and hurled it into another VTOL.

"What's the plan?"

"I won't be able to get in at all so we'll flush him out."

"And how exactly will we do that? If we attack he'll only stay put."

"Exactly."

"I don't understand."

"I'll explain."

It was simple yet effective. An old trick in the war book but with a twist. They can only determine the cause but not the total effect. As they approached the tower, it was heavily guarded as the pilot promised. A bombardment from the outside would prove futile and plain stupid. Any tactician would say-so or find a different conclusion as to why. Lazarus stood watch from another building.

"Alright Cat it's all up to you, don't disappoint," he thought.

Lazarus had great capabilities in stealth but Cat is by far the best. She is the only one who could pull this off.

Cat left her scythe in the VTOL. Its size and weight would prove cumbersome and would hinder her progress. Instead of that she used her claws. Cat was swift and quiet like her feline name. She could trail right behind a trooper and would have never been heard. When she couldn't go forward she had to go up. Her claws easily removed the cover to the air ducts and crawled through. She continued her way upward until the top floor was accessible. Disciple looked out the window while sitting in his chair. Pulse rifles sounded as did shouts of pain. Some type of weapon was tearing the guards to bits. The two closest to the door formed up. All the others had their rifles trained on the door. The doors slid apart and a figure stood. The triggers were pulled and the body jolted and jerked.

"Cease fire!" one commanded.

The corpse dropped to the floor riddled with holes and punctures. The troopers closest to the door were killed first. Cat easily maneuvered from one trooper to the next. Wounds were painfully torn open by those claws. She snatched the pistol of the one trooper and fired on him and two others. Cat threw the pistol at another trooper and attacked the other two. Their rifles were destroyed by her claws and she jabbed them in their throats. She quickly dashed towards the retaliating trooper and cut him down to size. A total of eight bodies lay on the ground. Cat flicked the blood off her claws as Disciple sat in his chair. The 'nonchalant' attitude didn't disappear from his face. "Not bad but I've seen better." Disciple moved in front of the desk. "A really dumb move to join sides with Lazarus."

"I'd rather be with Lazarus than be Onyx's slave." Disciple activated his arm blades.

"I am no slave! Onyx is more powerful than all of us combined!" He lounged at Cat who countered with a flip-kick. Her follow-up was a firm palm strike. Disciple crashed into the desk, "Don't try me Disciple."

Cat dodged a flying chair.

"Please Cat don't make me laugh."

"I must be on a roll tonight," she mumbled to herself.

Claws and blade clashed and clanged. Disciple was the youngest of them all which meant he had much to learn. Cat back-handed him and kicked him back. As Disciple recovered, Cat planted both feet into his face sending him out the window. Lazarus came from beneath and knocked him into the sky. He shaded above Disciple in the apex of his altitude and knocked him back to earth. Commuters ran away in fright as Disciple crashed upon the road. Lazarus wasn't far behind, two knees from him rammed into Disciple's chest. The impact kicked up dust and asphalt that pelted anything in range. Windows were shattered and cars were flipped over. Disciple was dead on impact. The dust finally settled and the body was visible. The indentations of where the knees impacted were clearly seen. It was sad to Lazarus that such a young man had to die. Cat stood next to Lazarus, "What's next?"

"Onyx and anyone else who is still loyal to him."

"Like him."

He dodged the hammer throw that knocked Cat into a building. She was down for the count. The hammer returned to his hand and swung at Lazarus.

"I forgot all about Chaos," he thought.

"Surprised to see me?"

"A lot actually, you're supposed to be dead Chaos."

Lazarus flipped into the sky and fired lightning bolts. Chaos blocked the bolts with his hammer.

"Maybe you're not as strong as you think you are."

"Hardly! What I can't figure out is how you recovered from such a clash?"

Lazarus deflected the hammer blows and threw Chaos back. Lazarus grabbed a car and hurled it at the hammer-wielder. One swing and the car was gone. Chaos rushed him with a barrage of attacks. The blows jarred him left and right. To weaker beings these blows would kill them. One final blow sent him to the ground.

"I can't believe you're even related to Onyx."

Chaos raised his hammer for one more crushing blow. Before the blow was dealt Lazarus shaded behind him. "You've been holding back," Chaos thought. "Don't tell me that you used up all of your energy."

He didn't deny the accusation at all.

"Allow me to show you true power."

Lazarus slammed his foot into his back sending him flying. He shaded in front of Chaos and kneed him in his stomach. Another blow sent him into a building. Bolts formed in both hands until each hand was side by side. The beautiful energy amounted in his hands until he released all of it. The terrifying beam of sparking energy streaked towards the hammer-wielder. "See you in hell, Chaos!"

The building erupted into a magnificent explosion. The people ran and screamed in fear. Excruciating heat blasted pass his armored body. That beam that could have ended the entire planet withered and dissipated. The firstborn breathed heavily, the power was both exhilarating and exhausting. When one is careless with that power then they have serious problems. Lazarus floated over to Cat who was covered in the rubble. She is a strong soul but her injuries were devastating. Her nimble frame was cradled in his arms as he floated away from the ruins of the building.

"Lord Lazarus we have a dire situation upon us."

"Admiral Tone, what is it?" This 'problem' doesn't sound too good to Lazarus.

"Chevalier is under siege."

"What?!"

"The evading force is led by Mercy in his flagship, *Summer's Dawn*."

"A dire situation indeed."

The Horseman

The fiery-red hooves continued down the beaten path. The rider would seem to be an angel from far. His silver-white hair and mystic-blue eyes could easily fool anyone from a distance. Only when he is near should one truly wallow in fear. Within that moment they will realize that this being is War, one of the four horsemen of the apocalypse. The horseman was larger than the average human, taller too. The armor he wore would easily crush any wearer of a lesser degree. Chaos, his trusty steed, snorted and snarled. "Greetings rider and welcome."

He stayed silent. "A quiet one I suppose, well at least tell me of your travel so far."

"It was a hard path and a dangerous path. It was crooked, lonely, and long."

"What is it you that you seek horseman."

"The valley of light," he said plainly.

"If that is what you seek then you are on the right path. You must continue through these mountains. Careful, there are strange things living in the pools and lakes in the heart of the mountains."

"Nothing I haven't dealt with in the past."

"Yes of course nothing discourages the great War."

"I'm not surprised that you know me but I don't know you."

It's true many did know of the riders.

"Where are my manners, I am Zalazar and I'm here to amuse your wares!"

"Another time merchant!"

He didn't yell at the merchant but he did make clear he didn't want to talk. War proceeded pass his new 'friend.' "Horseman, before you go take this." Zalazar handed War a talisman.

"It's a Pathfinder talisman so you'll never get lost."

War nodded his thanks and continued on without another word. He climbed the mountains fighting the bitter winds and unforgiving cold. War was no stranger to discomfort or quests in his millenniums of living. A horseman is immortal unless they are killed by the action of others. Such a thing is unheard of and if a horseman was killed one would have to break the final seal to revive him. War reigned his mount to a halt and inspected the entrance of the cave.

"This is the end for you my friend," War said as he dismounted.

Chaos stood upon his hind legs once more before vanishing. War marched into the cave with no worries. It was deep, deep and dark. Such as only goblins that have taken to living in the heart of the mountains can see through.

He waded deeper into the icy water until he was completely submerged and swam to the other side. The rushing wind signified an exit to the cave. War climbed out of the water and continued his journey. There was no need to summon Chaos he traveled far enough. Besides his owner is strong enough himself, he can make the distance. Good thing Zalazar gave him that talisman for conditions have gotten worse. War was caught in a tempest that was getting worse by the minute. The horseman has seen better days but he isn't complaining. He's a warrior and a warrior's life isn't easy, nor simple.

Lightning struck the peaks above causing massive boulders to fall into War's path.

"Go back?" he thought. "No good at all! Go sideways? Impossible. Go forward? Only thing to do! On I go!"

He picked up the pace breaking into a sprint. War did his best to dodge the boulders but the path is slim and the boulders were huge. Lightning struck once again, sending the biggest boulder tumbling into his path. He broke into an even faster sprint just to make it pass in time. "I'm not going to make it," War realized.

Despite his best effort he still wasn't fast enough, his armor held him back. The great strength War was known for surged through his entire body. He leapt through the darkness and rain and obliterated the boulder with a single punch. The boulder was nothing but dust that was washed away in the storm.

Arising from one knee he flexed his fist and continued his march. The storm continued for sometime longer until finally passing. "You have come to the very edge of the wild," War thought. The Red Rider was almost to the Valley of Light.

The forest was dry and warm, blossoming with ripe fruit. War would gladly stop and eat but he had a mission to complete. *Snap*. Suddenly an orc jumped out of nowhere seeking the rider's blood. The orc was knocked back by a powerful blow. Orcs jumped out and completely surrounded War. He looked left and right, not at the orcs but he searched for the one who struck the initial orc. His grip tightened around the hilt of his mighty sword, *Perdition*. His lip curled in distaste as the pale figure descended on another victim. The other orcs were startled by the howls of pain. War swung in high-arcs beheading two orcs and stabbing another. One horseman is a dangerous adversary but two back-to-back are unbeatable. It's a death sentence and the orcs experienced this first-hand.

The two riders displayed their superiority in this battle. No it's not a battle it's more of an exercise. These orcs weren't trained combatants, they were brawling savages that were being 'put down.' Ebony blade and jagged scythe destroyed the last of the adversaries. Once the imminent danger was gone they turned to face one another, "Why are you here Death?"

"I had to make sure you were getting the job done."

"You doubted my capabilities?"

"Come, tell me about your journey so far," his brother said. On they went walking and talking as brothers would normally do. War is more trusting and open when he's with his brother or any of his siblings. There are few people one could trust in this line of work.

The two riders were the same size but Death was cadaverous and had a skeletal physique. This is probably the reason why he can sustain immeasurable damage, near invulnerability. He is also the quickest of the four horsemen and one could never catch him off-guard. Death appears cold on the outside but deep on the inside he cared for his kin.

"We're here," War said.

They were so lost in speech and thought that they lost track. The valley was beautiful and vast, filled with fruit and vegetation. One could stay here forever if they chose to. This place is the result of divine work whether you believe it or not. The two horsemen pulled their terrible weapons.

"You sensed them as well," Death said.

Heavily-armed angels descended out of the sky and aimed their halberds at the riders. The two brothers made quick work of the angels. "I remembered angels being tougher," War said.

Yet, another one crashed to the ground. They turned to face the gold-winged angel, an Archangel. "You don't belong here horsemen so this is your only chance to turn away and leave."

"Uriel you know we can't do that. You guard a portal to Earth which is forbidden. I will destroy that portal."

"Not as long as I live."

War smirked at her comment, "So be it."

Death drove the haft of Damnation, his potent scythe, into the ground and leaned against it. They charged and greeted one another's blade. Uriel was a formidable opponent, to others. She was clearly no match for the horseman, he has been alive for far too long. Uriel was well trained and experienced, no doubt giving War a fight. War dashed to the side just dodging a lethal stroke. *"Yes, she has gained much power since the last time we met. How many centuries ago was that?"* War thought to himself. He swung Perdition in high-arching loops until horseman and archangel met in a 'blade lock.' Uriel was strong but she couldn't match War's strength. War worked the sword out of her hand and rammed his fist in her chest sending the archangel crashing into the rocks. Uriel was defeated and nearly passed out, she was no longer a threat. Blood trickled from her mouth as she sat there breathing heavily.

"Come back in a millennium or two then you could pose a threat."

Death clapped his hands together in approval. "Only few can beat an Archangel let alone make them bleed."

War smiled for the first time in a very long time. "Let's not over stay our welcome here," War said.

The red rider destroyed the portal to the kingdom of man and started to leave. Uriel attempted to stand up but fell to her knees, too weak to even crawl. "So an Archangel was the reason why evil things did not come into this valley."

"Now she's too weak to protect it," Death added, "Won't be long until some orcs come by and notice the fruit and vulnerable angel."

"We can't just leave her here, she's strong but she doesn't possess the power we do."

"First you try to kill her but now you find sympathy? War I will never understand you."

Death stared off into the distance for a moment, "fine but you have to carry her."

War proceeded to pick up the angel, "Away from me horseman!"

"Quiet angel before I change my mind." She wasn't going to be quiet at all.

"What did I get myself into."

War Machine

"The prototype is said to be unstoppable."

"Yeah that's why most clans are gone now."

The sound of the machine hummed as it powered up. "Where are they sending us anyway?" Pandora asked.

The machine was at full power and the two fighters were teleported to a distant planet.

"Here."

The war machine had torn a path into the village. The fire and smoke filled the night sky choking its beauty.

"Prototype? This thing is a monster!"

Beings appeared wearing some form of a combat skin. It's similar to the type Cerrius and Pandora wear. The difference was in the armament and its weight. It is military grade for increased protection against ballistics and concussive forces. The fighters wear combat skin that is lighter and more flexible so they can move faster and are more agile. Weapons were pointed at Cerrius and Pandora.

"Who are you?!" The demented voice was obviously angry.

"I'm Cerrius and this is Pandora."

"Why are you here?! Are you here to inflict more pain?!" yelled the commander.

"No, we're here to stop that thing." He pointed at the war-path.

The sound of combat could be heard by both the humans and the Spectrain.

"Well now is your chance."

They stopped at the edge of the hill.

"There it is, there's Ares," one of the Spectra's said.

Ares was a befitting name for the machine. The spectras fired at Ares with no effect. The machine demolished the aliens with his fists alone. It was pure savagery. Ares upper-cutted one spectra out of sight.

"That's gotta hurt," Pandora winced.

"Ares is very powerful and one hit could kill either one of us."

"You're not cheering me up Cerrius."

"That's our advantage, with all that strength his agility is out of the window," Cerrius added.

The last of the spectrains were destroyed.

"Let's go."

Cerrius and Pandora leaped in front of the prototype, Ares attacked immediately. Cerrius directed War Machine's fist into the ground and jabbed Ares in his chin. Pandora jammed both escrima sticks into his neck, electrocuted him, and kneed his face. The tabletop maneuver placed Ares on the ground.

He grabbed both fighters by the throat and stood. Ares slammed both of them together. "This is going to be tougher than I thought," said Cerrius.

They synchronized their high-kicks releasing them from the grasp of death. Cerrius threw two shurikens that exploded on impact. He then assaulted his abdomen with a barrage of punches. Ares absorbed the assault from Cerrius until he caught his arm. He hurled Cerrius into Pandora causing the two of them to fall. Cerrius stopped the crushing boot but not for long. He twisted the foot bringing Ares to a knee. Pandora slipped from underneath him and kicked Ares in the face. He grabbed her leg and threw Pandora nice and far. Ares then buried his fist into Cerrius' stomach causing him to double over. The spectras intervened before the prototype could finish the job. Ares turned to deal with the spectras. "Cerrius are you okay?"

He caught his second-wind and stood.

"I guess one punch won't kill you."

"It almost did, his fist is the size of your head Pandora."

Ares finished the spectras and disappeared.

"He's gone."

The two of them searched the corpses until one was found still breathing. Pandora kneeled beside him and cradled his head. It was the commander who first spoke to them. His chest was caved in and was filling with blood.

"You," he pointed at Pandora, "Earthling must stop that infernal machine."

"How?"

"You'll find out when the time is right."

He had his final breath before passing away. She closed his eyes and laid him back down. "Cerrius, I don't know how to stop that thing."

Her escrima sticks now rested on her lower back. "You saw him, you saw how he threw me."

The mentor adjusted his gauntlets, "You're right, I did see that throw."

Cerrius started to check the rest of the bodies.

"We'll have to be relentless like Ares. Techniques mixed with savagery should do damage."

"So you propose that we stoop to his level?"

"Sometimes you have to."

Cerrius analyzed the trail left behind, "C'mon."

Pandora hacked into the spectrain military-coded frequencies. This allowed them to hear what the spectrains hear.

"You said savagery, right?" said Pandora.

"Yes savagery."

The grass rustled underneath their boots. It was a beautiful place with grassy-knolls and trees. It's a nice place to visit but it was no place for a human to live. Nothing against planet Ontario-Mathis at all, there's just no place like home.

"I said, Savagery, because you can't hold back with such an opponent. If you want to beat this machine you'll need every ounce of savagery you have."

Chatter shot through their comm-links. There was coded military talk for saying *a village was under attack*.

Ares rampaged through the village killing anything in its way. The spectras were no match for the unrestrained might. Corpses laid on the ground broken and shattered. More arrived only to be added to the corpses. A shuriken exploded on the back of his head. Pandora once again electrocuted him but this time it had no effect. She stayed low and dodged the attacks.

Pandora connected her sticks to form her escrima staff. The results of chaining her attacks together gave Cerrius enough time to follow up. He unleashed a furious attack on Ares.

Technique and savagery used in unison is very effective, and very dangerous. If one isn't careful he can lose control and go off the deep-end. Ares countered one blow and body-slammed Cerrius. The entire ground shook from the brute force.

Pandora quickly reacted with a knock-back technique. Ares absorbed the blow and whipped the young fighter into an awaiting shack.

Ares checked both fighters who were down for the count. Seeing that they no longer pose a threat the savage machine left.

The village was desolate and filled with silence. The inhabitants who survived emerged from their hiding places. The menace had left leaving nothing but despair and corpses behind. Pandora stumbled through the rubble as Cerrius, too, came to his senses.

Both fighters were on their feet and assessing the current situation. "I now know why most clans have failed."

Pandora agreed with Cerrius as they caught their breath. The Spectrains were hospitable and offered the two of them a place to stay.

After they lost and allowed an insane prototype to destroy their village the Spectrains still offered them a place to rest. "This, *God of War*, just might be invincible."

Ares might have knocked some screws loose in Cerrius' head. "My first use of the electro-shocks nearly fried Ares. The second time he just shrugged it off."

Pandora shook her head, "I don't know if you've been paying attention to our last engagements but that strategy isn't working."

Cerrius leaned back in his chair, "Do you propose something different?"

"A theory."

Cerrius sighed, "Pandora…"

"Just hear me out. In Greek Mythology the God of War, Ares, receives his power from conflict."

"I'm listening," said Cerrius nodding his head.

"When he is 'starved', in a sense, his powers are relatively weak."

Cerrius cocked his head.

"This prototype of ours feeds off the conflict and chaos it creates. That's why he could shrug off the attack the second time."

"What is it you want us to do, nothing?"

"Exactly."

Pandora sat back in her chair confident in her theory. It was quite good and reasonable.

"Pandora you have no idea how dangerous that theory is. What if your theory backfires and Ares kills you?"

"At times the hardest thing to do is to turn the other cheek."

Cerrius shook his head, "No, no, I'm not letting you do this."

They could hear the military chatter once again. No doubt it was Ares. He was closing in on a major city. The Spectras were failing and were calling for reinforcements. The two of them were out the door.

Ares' campaign of chaos led him towards the city. The Spectras held their ground but it was futile. One-hit blows destroyed entire platoons now. His power dramatically increased since the last encounter. It would sharply increase if he entered the city. Ares marched through the wall of incoming fire. The Spectras inched back as they did their best to stop the monster.

"Hold your fire!" one of them yelled.

Pandora stood in front of the Spectras. They continued to aim at Ares. Cerrius finally caught up. Spectras held him back as the war machine approached Pandora. His footsteps could cause an earthquake. The unstoppable force met the immovable object head on. Ares stopped in front of tiny Pandora. He scanned her over and classified her as a threat.

She dropped her staff and stood as tall as she could.

"Get out of the way!"

Cerrius struggled to get pass the strong-armed Spectras. The others trembled as they continued to aim at Ares. His arms, that had the power to level entire buildings, slowly rose to crush Pandora.

"You don't understand! A single blow can kill her, she isn't strong enough!"

His heart nearly pounded out of his chest. The Spectrain forces slowly lowered their weapons not knowing exactly why. Pandora was determined to stop Ares, even if the price was her life. Ares eyes flickered, the more he lowered his arms the more his eyes flickered.

Cerrius' heart was nearly on the ground as a million things raced through his mind. He wanted to throw a shuriken but something, some invisible force, held him back.

Ares' arms slowed to a pause and his eyes faded to black.

The war machine was offline.

www.ingramcontent.com/pod-product-compliance
Lightning Source LLC
Chambersburg PA
CBHW071217130626
46555CB00004B/1739